How to Catch Santa

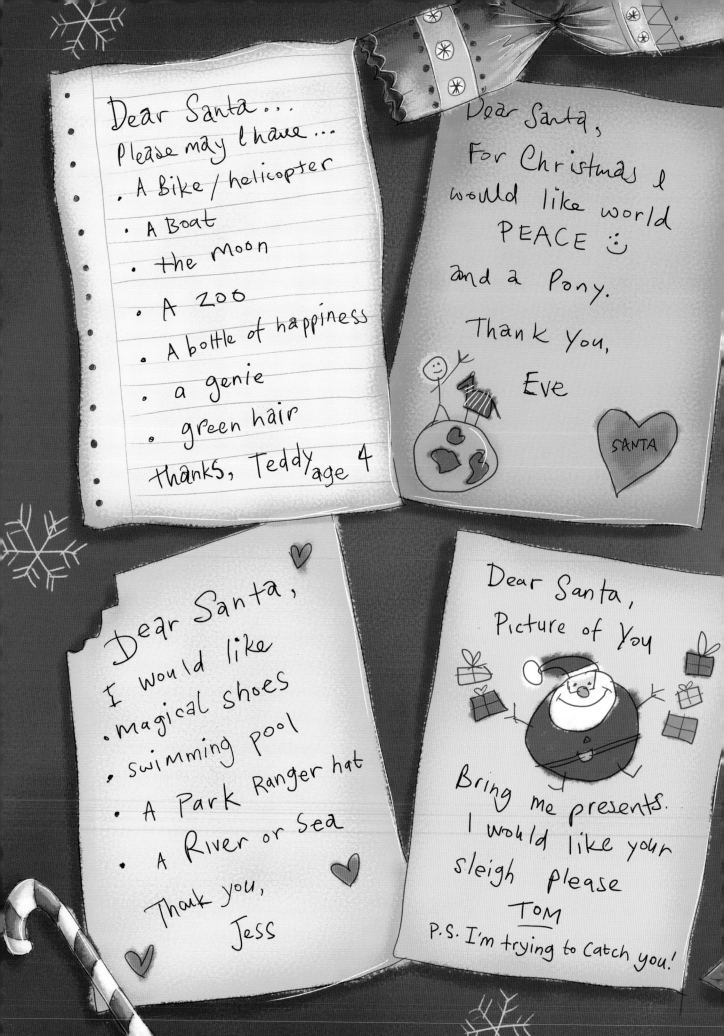

Dear Santa...
Please may I have...
. A bike / helicopter
. A Boat
. the Moon
. A ZOO
. A bottle of happiness
. a genie
. green hair
thanks, Teddy age 4

Dear Santa,
For Christmas I
would like world
PEACE :)
and a Pony.
Thank You,
Eve

SANTA

Dear Santa,
I would like
. magical shoes
. swimming pool
. A Park Ranger hat
. A River or Sea
Thank you,
Jess

Dear Santa,
Picture of You

Bring me presents.
I would like your
sleigh please
TOM
P.S. I'm trying to Catch you!

Dear Santa,
I would like...
- $ 20,000,000,000
- 1 shooting star
- spaceship
- Tiger
- New longer Arms

    Carl

Dear Santa,
I would be very happy if you could bring me...
a cloud.
or a Doll's house.
    Thank you,
        Tilly

Dear Santa,
I would like
a robot and
x-ray eyes for
Christmas please
also if you have time
bionic legs....
        Jerry

DEAR SANTA,
I would like
the best present
in the world...
please keep this
letter and reuse
for the next year!
        Sam

Dear Santa,
anything but
Socks. thanks,
        Dad

How to Catch Santa

BY JEAN REAGAN

ILLUSTRATED BY LEE WILDISH

DRAGONFLY BOOKS — NEW YORK

For my niece, Judy, and for all my hiking
and critique buddies. Thank you! —J.R.

Merry Christmas, Ivy, Oscar, Grace, and Laura —L.W.

Text copyright © 2015 by Jean Reagan
Cover art and interior illustrations copyright © 2015 by Lee Wildish

All rights reserved.
Published in the United States by Dragonfly Books, an imprint of Random House Children's Books,
a division of Penguin Random House LLC, New York. Originally published in hardcover in the United States by Alfred A. Knopf,
an imprint of Random House Children's Books, a division of Penguin Random House LLC, New York, in 2015.

Dragonfly Books and colophon are registered trademarks of Penguin Random House LLC.

Visit us on the Web! rhcbooks.com

Educators and librarians, for a variety of teaching tools, visit us at RHTeachersLibrarians.com

The Library of Congress has cataloged the hardcover edition of this work as follows:
Reagan, Jean.
How to catch Santa / by Jean Reagan ; illustrated by Lee Wildish. — First edition.
pages cm.
Summary: A child provides instructions for properly capturing Santa—briefly—to ask him questions and tell him things.
ISBN 978-0-553-49839-4 (trade) — ISBN 978-0-553-49840-0 (lib. bdg.) — ISBN 978-0-553-49841-7 (ebook)
I. Santa Claus—Juvenile fiction. [1. Santa Claus—Fiction. 2. Christmas—Fiction.] I. Wildish, Lee, illustrator. II. Title.
PZ7.R2354Hp 2015
[E]—dc23
2014025428

ISBN 978-0-593-30190-6 (pbk.)

MANUFACTURED IN CHINA
10 9 8 7 6 5 4
First Dragonfly Books Edition

After waiting for days and days and *days*, it's finally
Christmas Eve.
And *that's* when you can try to catch Santa.

As you know, Santa's very busy, and you won't be able to keep him for long. So plan ahead. Figure out *now* how to make the most of your time.

First of all, don't you have a zillion questions to ASK him?

QUESTIONS FOR SANTA:

How do you squeeze down chimneys?

How do you stay clean?

What about houses with no chimneys?

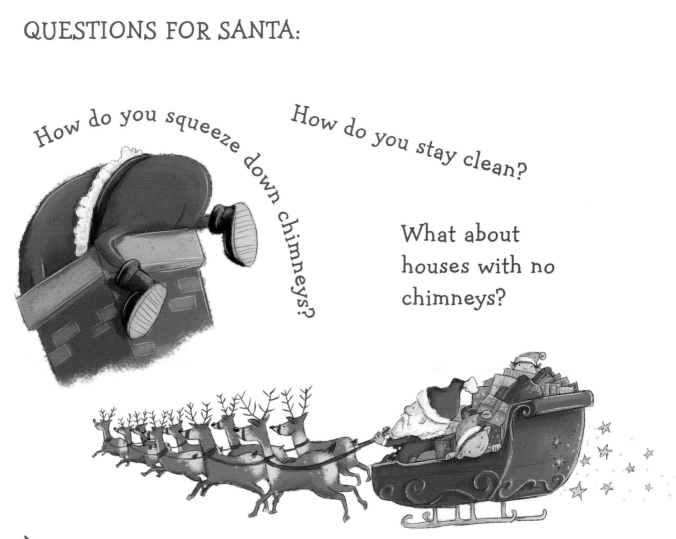

How fast do reindeer fly to get everywhere in one night?

What's their fuel? Magic?

Do elves ever sneak a ride in your sleigh?
What about kids?

How do you find kids who are away on trips?

What's *your* favorite toy?

Do you get mountains and **mountains** of letters?

Who invents new toys
at your workshop?

The elves?

Mrs. Claus?

You?

Do you really eat cookies at everyone's house?

Maybe you have things you want to TELL him.

THINGS TO TELL SANTA:

I'm trying very hard to be good.
My sister is, too, even if it doesn't look like it.

Thank you for the presents!
Sorry I always forget to send a thank-you note.

I know what my mom and dad want.
They were too busy to write to you.

And maybe you have things you want to GIVE him.
(Santa will *love* that!)

THINGS TO GIVE
SANTA:

A headlamp for going
down dark, dark chimneys

A nose warmer for
cold sleigh rides

Drawings of
Santa with
your family

Homemade Christmas
decorations for Mrs. Claus

Okay, now you know what you'll do once you catch Santa. It's time to figure out HOW to do it. Definitely don't try anything too WILD AND CRAZY:

Lassoing Santa

Distracting him with a giant candy cane

Luring him into a snow trap

Tying nets between palm trees

Instead: Be crafty! Be clever! Be *gentle*!

If you're very lucky, you will *actually catch Santa*. But you might only catch a *glimpse* of him. Or you might just find "Santa's been here" clues.

PLAN FOR ALL THESE POSSIBILITIES:

Early on Christmas Eve, write Santa a note and fill it with glitter.

When he opens it, glitter will sprinkle all over him and he'll leave a trail. That's a "Santa's been here" clue for sure.

Scatter carrots in your yard or on the windowsill.

If they disappear, that's a "reindeer have been here" clue!

Write Santa riddles, but
DON'T GIVE THE ANSWERS! (Yet.)

RIDDLES
?
FOR SANTA.

Bake him cookies.

Instead of putting them by the tree, draw arrows leading to your room.

String bells and chimes above the cookies.

That way, he'll make a racket and wake you up.

Now try to be patient. While you wait, sing Christmas songs and read books about Santa. Maybe you'll even get some new Santa-catching ideas.

Ask your mom and dad if they ever tried to catch Santa when they were little. Do they have any tricks? Check with your grandma and grandpa, too.

When it starts to get dark, Santa and his reindeer begin
their rounds. Have everyone keep an eye out the window.

If your family makes lots of noise—laughing, eating, talking, playing games—say "*Shhhhhh!*" every now and then and listen for Santa sounds. . . .

SANTA SOUNDS:

Santa doing stretches
on your neighbor's roof

Sleigh bells

"Ho, Ho, HO!"

Reindeer whinnying
in the distance

Elves giggling

When you start to get sleepy,
MAKE LAST-MINUTE PREPARATIONS:

Leave the Christmas tree lights on
to help Santa see his way around.

Rudolph-with-his-nose-so-bright can't help him from the roof.

Set out your Santa riddles with a note
that says "For help with the answers,
wake me up."

Santa won't be able to resist!

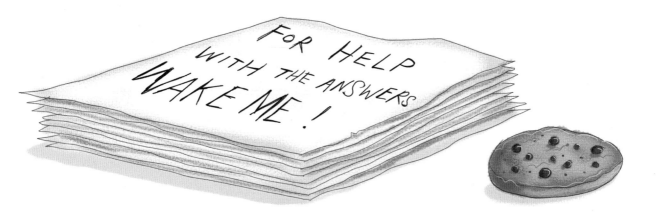

Is your puppy a good watchdog?
A good, *gentle* watchdog? If yes,
then let him stay in your bedroom.

Remember, Santa won't come to your
house until you're asleep.

Before you lay your head on your
pillow, peek out the window one
last time.

Good luck catching Santa, and . . .

And if you didn't catch Santa this time,
don't worry. There's always next year. . . .

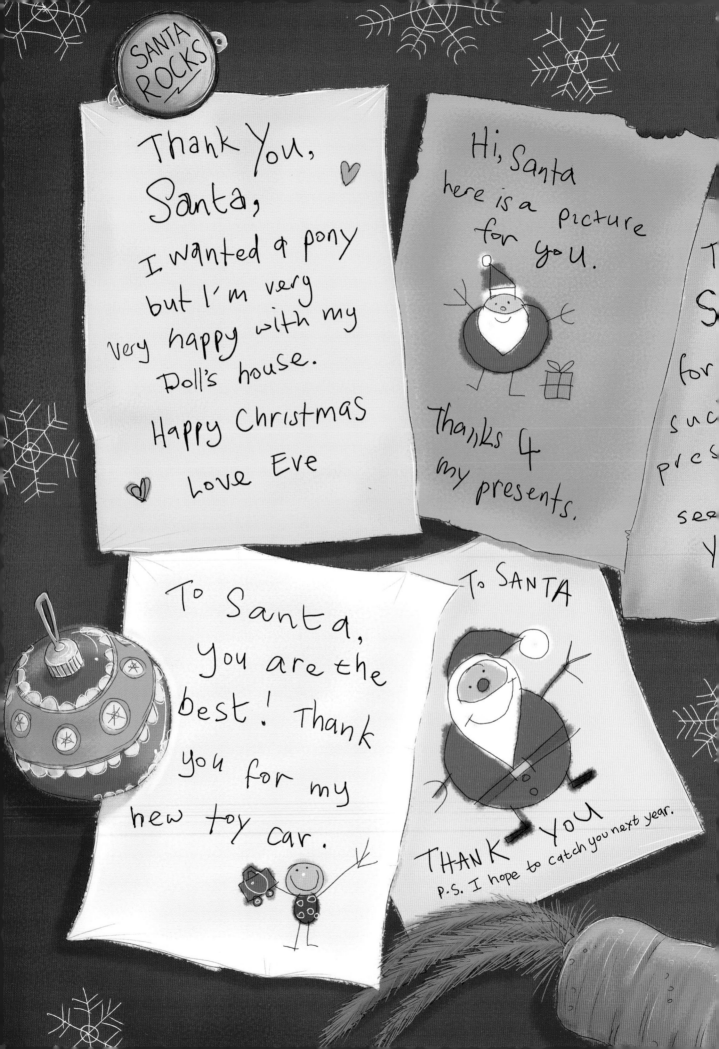

Dear Santa,
I wish you a lovely Christmas.

thank you very much for all the fantastic presents.

Thanks

TO SANTA
I like your beard.
Thank you for the presents.

TO SANTA,
I want to thank you for my presents. My cat likes his too. Here is a drawing of him.

TO SANTA
Thank You for my beautiful presents

Thanks for all the socks, Santa.
Dad